First I win a contest
that makes me a reality
TV star. Then I get to
do some of the most
awesome extreme sports
in the world. And my
two best friends get to
come along for the ride.
How lucky am I?

Wellington (Aust.) Pty Ltd
ABN 30 062 365 413
433 Wellington Street
Clifton Hill
VIC 3068
AUSTRALIA

www.kidzbookhub.com.au

Distributed by Amba Press.

Print ISBN: 978-1-925308-75-4
eBook ISBN: 978-1-925308-76-1

A catalogue record for this
work is available from the
National Library of Australia

THE XTREME WORLD OF

BILLY KOOL

BOOK 7
KART RACING

BY
PHIL KETTLE

CONTENTS

KART EQUIPMENT

Driving Shoes

Driving shoes have special soles that help you grip the accelerator and the brake.

Helmet

A special aerodynamic helmet is needed to reduce drag and protect your head, in case of an accident.

Racing Tyres

Racing tyres grip the road like Formula One tyres.

SSC Racing Kart

The SSC Racing Kart is like a miniature Formula One car. It goes very fast and is low to the ground for fast cornering.

Gloves

Gloves help drivers grip the steering wheel. They are made out of materials such as leather and suede.

Racing Suit

There is the risk you may fall out so you need to protect your body with a full-length racing suit.

MY POP

On Monday after school, Dad told me that my grandfather was coming to stay with us. I was totally rapt.

I hoped for a minute that he might be coming to live with us, but Dad said that Pop was only coming to stay for a week. Ever since my grandma died last year, my pop has lived on his own. I know that Pop sometimes gets lonely. I guess it must be strange for him living on his own. My pop and grandma had lived together in the same house for fifty years. The house must feel pretty big to him now.

I tried to spend as much time with him as I could. I've always thought of Pop as more of a friend than just my pop.

I've always been able to tell him everything — sometimes things that I didn't even tell my parents. Pop told me that now that he was a grandfather he had the time to be the father that he never was when my dad was young. I kind of knew what he was saying. I loved my dad heaps, but sometimes when I really wanted to do something with him, he was way too busy with his work.

Pop told me that when he was my dad's age, he was just the same.

'It's really difficult when you're working,' he said. 'Sometimes you have to do work things when you would rather be spending time with your family.'

Pop helped me understand a lot of things that I had trouble with.

Pop was really the only person I had ever told that I sometimes thought I wasn't good enough to do the extreme sports we had to do for the show. He told me that if I really wanted to do something then I just had to believe that I could, and I'd be able to.

'Believe in yourself,' he said. 'Chase your dreams. There's a good chance that they could come true.'

Every time I had doubts about something I was doing, I thought about what Pop had said to me. That always seemed to make me try harder.

After every show Pop would ring me up to tell me how great the show was. He was really proud of what I was doing. He had even rung Nathan and Sally to tell them how good they were.

Pop thought it was fantastic that I was doing extreme sports. He always told me that having fun sometimes meant taking risks. It was great that Pop was coming to stay with us in the week that our extreme sport was kart racing. Pop had built me my first billy-kart.

Not only that, he taught me how to fish. He even let Nathan come with us. Nathan thinks Pop is great, too.

I really liked going fishing with Pop. I liked it more for the stories that he told when we were fishing, than the actual fishing itself. He told me all about the things he did when he was my age.

Of course, according to Pop, everything that he did back then was better than what we do now. He called the time when he was young, the 'olden days'.

When I told Dad about some of the things that Pop told me, Dad said, 'Remember, the older people get, the better they were.'

I sort of knew what he meant.

COMING TO STAY

When I got home from school on Tuesday afternoon, my pop's car was parked in the garage. Pop had owned the same car for thirty years. It was his pride and joy. He must have polished the car every week. Sometimes I helped him. There wasn't a single mark on the car, except for the one near the front bumper bar. But my pop didn't put that ding in his car. I did!

Pop taught me to drive. I'm sure my parents would have done a total flip if they had ever found out, but Pop took his car out of the garage and backed it down the driveway. He then put a box on the seat and told me to drive the car to the garage.

We spent all that morning driving the car thirty metres to the garage and then reversing it back down the driveway.

By the end of the morning I was ready to be a racing car driver. I was planning a career in Formula One for when I left school. It was during the last drive toward the garage that I must have become too confident. I must have been going a little too fast. When I went to put my foot on the brake, I hit the accelerator. The car leapt forward and went straight through the garage doors, knocking them open. I hit the brake, the tyres skidded, and the car pulled up just before the back wall of the garage. The metal rubbish bin that was resting against the back wall was no longer round. It was as flat as a pancake.

Pop said that was the end of the

driving lessons for the day. I thought that he would have been really upset. But he wasn't. He said that sometimes you had to pay a price for learning some things and that a small ding was a small price. He suggested maybe that we should keep it our little secret and not tell my parents about what had happened. That was fine by me.

THE TALK

Pop said that he was only going to stay till after next weekend. He said that he would have to leave then so that he could catch the train home. I asked him why he was catching the train home and not driving his car.

He looked at Mum and Dad — he had a sad look on his face. He said he wanted to go for a walk and asked if I wanted to come because he wanted to talk to me.

'I've got something that I want to give you,' Pop said as he handed me a key.

'What's this for?' I asked.

'This is the key to my car ... I mean this is the key to your car,' he said.

'But this is your car,' I said.

'It's your car now,' he said.

'But I'm too young to drive and what are you going to do for a car?'

'You might be too young to drive, but I'm too old to drive,' Pop said.

I didn't know what to say. Pop looked smaller than he ever had. His shoulders were hunched and he was walking very slowly.

When we got home, I went into my bedroom and rang Shey. I told her what my pop had done. Shey said that I should bring Pop kart racing on the weekend. I really wanted Pop to know that he wasn't too old. He always told me that you should never give up. I knew that if he gave me his car, he was giving up. I didn't want my pop to give up.

CAST AND CREW MEETING

On Friday the limo picked us up for the cast and crew meeting. Sally, Nathan and I talked Pop into coming to the studio.

After we'd hassled him for ages, he said that he would come but he still wasn't sure about racing. He said, 'My driving days are over. But when I was younger I think I could have been a champion racing car driver.'

When Nathan asked him why he hadn't become a champion racing car driver, he just smiled and said, 'When I was a boy there wasn't a car invented that was fast enough for me'.

Nathan said that he couldn't wait to race. 'It'll be the first step to becoming a Formula One driver.'

'Well, I hope that you drive a kart better than you ride a mountain bike or you'll never finish the race,' said Sally.

Everyone was really excited to meet Pop when we got to the meeting. They all shook hands with him. The director said, 'I hope I'm still racing karts when I'm your age, Mr Kool.'

Pop straightened his shoulders and asked what he had to do during the filming.

'We'll have kart-cams attached to the karts,' the director said. 'And there'll be two camera crews around the track. You'll all be wired for sound. We'll have all the safety equipment ready for you when you get to the track tomorrow. So all you have to do, Mr Kool, is try to beat these kids around the track.'

'I think I can do that,' Pop said.

'This will be a great episode,' the director said. 'The limo will pick you up at nine tomorrow.'

PROD: BILLY KOOL   CAM: 3

DIR: TAKE:

ROLL: SLATE: #1

#1   #6

DATE:

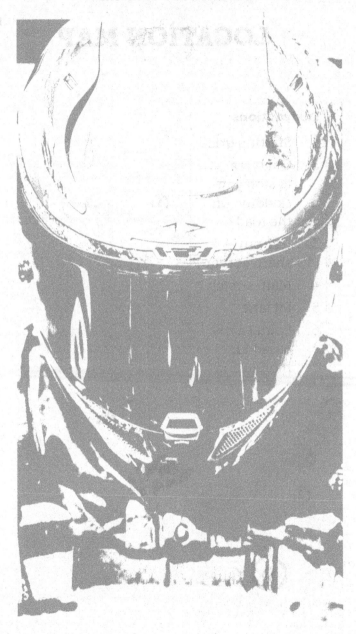

LOCATION MAP

Instructions

1. Starting grid
2. Old tyres to stop you skidding off the road
3. Hairpin — sharp corner
4. Main stretch
5. Pit lane
6. Sound crew based for monitoring

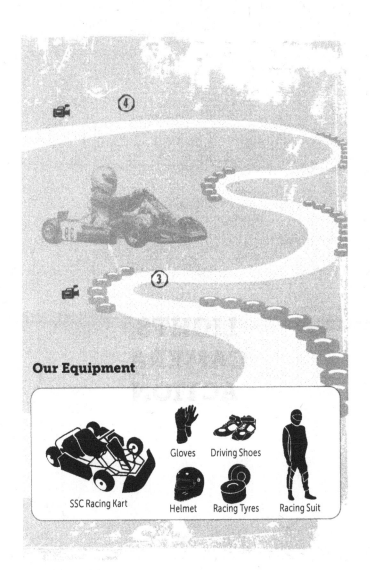

Our Equipment

SSC Racing Kart

Gloves

Driving Shoes

Helmet

Racing Tyres

Racing Suit

LIGHTS, CAMERA, ACTION

BILLY

Hi and welcome to *The Xtreme World Of Billy Kool*. My name is Billy Kool and as usual my co-hosts Nathan and Sally are with me. Today we are standing at the racing track. Our extreme sport today is kart racing.

NATHAN

Hi, Billy, and viewers. It's great to be here today. I can't wait to get on the track and burn some rubber.

SALLY

Good morning, everyone. And good morning to you, Nathan and Billy.

BILLY

Kart racing is one of the best adrenaline sports you can do. Did you know that most of the world's Formula One racing drivers started by racing karts?

NATHAN

That's why I think that if there's a Formula One racing team watching, they'll offer me a contract after today.

SALLY

Yeah, right, whatever.

BILLY

As usual, our safety co-ordinator, Shey, is also with us. Before we started filming today's show, we did some practice laps of the racetrack. Shey was really good.

SHEY

Thank you, Billy. Today is really special for me. Kart racing is my favourite extreme sport. The best thing about extreme kart racing is that you get to go so fast and are so close to the ground.

BILLY

Today is really special for me too. I would like to introduce my pop. Pop is going to prove to everyone that extreme sports can be enjoyed by people of all ages.

POP walks to where BILLY, NATHAN, SALLY and SHEY are standing. He is wearing a driving suit, and he looks nervous and excited.

POP

Where do I stand and where do I look?

BILLY

Just stand next to me and look at the camera!

Pop smiles at the camera.

19

SHEY

So, Mr Kool, do you think that you'll be the fastest around the track?

POP

I'm not too sure about that. I just hope that I get around the track without having an accident.

BILLY

I reckon that you'll probably be the fastest and best driver — after me of course.

SHEY

It's time to get into our karts and find out how good we are.

BILLY

The karts that we are using are special SSC racing karts.

SALLY

And what does SSC stand for?

BILLY

I have no idea.

NATHAN

I think it means that the karts can go really fast!

SHEY

When we're racing, it's good to wear protective clothing.

SALLY

As you can see we have driving suits on.

BILLY

We're also wearing helmets.

NATHAN

We're also wearing gloves that will help us hold the steering wheel. Kart racing can get bumpy.

POP

We've also got special shoes on. We all look like we've just come from outer space.

SHEY

We're going to race for four laps. First person over the finishing line wins. It's time to get into our karts and start the engines.

POP, SHEY, SALLY, NATHAN and BILLY get into their karts and start the engines. The karts move toward the starting line. The starting marshal moves into position and prepares to wave the chequered flag.

BILLY

This is how it must feel for the drivers in Formula One racing, when they line up on the grid.

NATHAN

I feel like I'm about to travel at the speed of light.

SALLY

When both of you have crashed into the edge of the track, I'll still be going around the track. So will Pop.

POP

I'm not too sure about this, Billy.

The starter raises the flag above his head. The motors of the karts scream. The starter brings the flag down. The race begins. The karts race off from the starting line.

BILLY

This is the first of the four laps. I'm in front, but Nathan's close behind me.

NATHAN

All our karts have exactly the same engine size.

SALLY

That means that the winner will be the driver that has the best skills.

The karts go down the straight. BILLY first, NATHAN second, SALLY third, SHEY fourth, POP fifth. POP is gaining on SHEY.

POP

These karts are really flying.

NATHAN

It feels as if I'm travelling at a million kilometres per hour.

24

BILLY

That's because the karts are so close to the ground! Are you having a good time, Pop?

POP

I should have done this years ago.

NATHAN and BILLY get through the first corner without mishap. They zoom off.

SALLY

Watch out, I'm going into the corner.

SHEY

So am I. Make sure you leave enough room for me.

SHEY and SALLY's karts reach the corner at the same time. POP is close behind.

25

SALLY hasn't slowed enough to take the corner. Her kart goes straight through the corner and crashes into the old tyres that line the edge of the track. She heads off SHEY's kart and SHEY is forced to drive into the old tyres as well. POP makes it through and sets off after BILLY and NATHAN.

SALLY

Sorry, Shey. I just lost it. I didn't slow down enough to go into the corner. I've lost a lot of ground. But I'm going to try and come back.

SHEY

No worries. All's fair in love and kart racing!

SALLY and SHEY manoeuvre their karts out of the tyre barrier and begin driving again. BILLY and NATHAN have

26

completed their first lap. POP is right on their tails as BILLY goes into a corner.

BILLY

My back wheels are slipping and sliding. This is where you really test your skills as a driver. Look out! I'm doing a massive spin out.

BILLY's kart starts to spin. The back end of the kart slides around — the kart is now facing the oncoming karts. NATHAN reaches the corner at the same time as BILLY.

NATHAN

Get out of the way! I'm going to stack straight into you, Billy.

CRASH! The two karts collide. POP goes wide and races past them.

POP

See you later, boys. Now it's time for me to show you all how a good driver races their kart.

BILLY

Go Pop! Lucky we've got all the right safety gear on, Nathan.

NATHAN

Yeah, that's for sure.

SALLY and SHEY catch up to BILLY and NATHAN, and pass them.

NATHAN

We are so far behind.

BILLY

Don't worry about me — I'm making a comeback.

SHEY

These karts have got more power than you think and it takes a lot of skill to drive them.

SALLY

I thought it would be like racing dodgem cars.

BILLY and NATHAN get their karts going again. NATHAN races into a corner. Again, his kart spins out of control and he comes to a stop.

POP

You can't put your foot on the brake when you're in the corner or you will lose control.

BILLY

I knew you'd be the best driver, Pop.

POP is well in front. SHEY is coming second, with SALLY close behind her. BILLY is half a lap behind them, and NATHAN is a full lap behind them.

SALLY

This is awesome. I really feel like a racing driver.

POP

I haven't had so much fun since ... well, I can't remember when I have ever had so much fun.

SHEY

You're nearly at the finishing line, Mr Kool.

POP

I've passed it!

BILLY

You won, Pop! That proves that you're still a great driver.

POP

Well, maybe I can still drive for a few more years yet.

BILLY/NATHAN/SALLY/SHEY

Of course you can!

NATHAN

Now we're racing for second place. May the second-best driver win!

SALLY and SHEY are head-to-head as they race down the final straight. It's impossible to tell who's in front.

SALLY

Ahhhhhhhhh! This is awesome.

POP

It's a photo finish!

SALLY's kart crosses the line a few centimetres in front of SHEY's.

SHEY

Good race, Sally!

SALLY

Hurry up, Billy and Nathan. Let's go again.

BILLY overtakes NATHAN on the straight and crosses the finishing line.

NATHAN

No way did I come last. We have to race again.

BILLY drives his kart into the pit lane. He gets out of the kart and takes his helmet off.

BILLY

While the others do a few practice laps, it's time for me to wind up the show. Maybe Pop will be able to give Nathan and me a few tips on how to take the corners.

I've had the best time racing karts. I'm sure that I will soon be back here racing again. On behalf of Nathan, Sally and all the crew, thank you for watching our show. Remember, extreme sports are the real thing. My name is Billy Kool. See you soon.

DIRECTOR

Cut! Well done. That was a great show. Now one of you bring your kart into the pit. I want to have a drive.

BILLY

I've got to get back out on the track. I reckon that I'm a better driver than they are — now I just have to prove it.

POP

Hurry up, Billy, and get back out onto the track. Fancy letting your grandfather beat you.

BILLY

Well, we'll just have to see about that.

NATHAN

This is awesome. I'm finally getting the hang of the corners. Oh-oh! No I'm not.

SALLY

None of you are as good as me.

EVERYONE

Yeah, right.

DIRECTOR

Okay, Shey, bring your kart in. I want to have a go.

SHEY

What was that? I can't hear you above the noise of the engines. It's so loud out here.

DIRECTOR

I said, bring your kart in. I want a go.

SHEY

Sorry. I have no idea what you just said.

DIRECTOR

Billy? Sally? Nathan? Mr Kool?

EVERYONE

What was that?

DIRECTOR

I said ... oh, just forget it. You're all acting like you're six years old. Even you, Mr Kool.

THE WRAP UP

I'm glad that my pop taught me to drive. With a bit more practice, I'm sure I could end up being a Formula One driver.

Nathan reckons that he's better than me. But he has to learn how to go around corners a lot better than he did.

Pop's decided that he is still able to drive his car. That's really good! He told me that on the next holidays we might go for a big road trip. Pop told me that the car is still mine, but he wants to drive it for a while yet. By the time he's really ready to stop driving it, I'll be ready to start. My pop is really cool!

Dear Billy

Do you think that you will be doing
more shows next year? If you don't,
I will be really upset!
Can you send me a selfie of you
with Nathan and Sally?

Caitlin, one of your biggest fans

EXTREME
INFORMATION

History

Since the invention of the first go-kart in 1956, kart racing has become more and more popular all over the world.

One of the biggest reasons for this is that people of all different ages can get involved in go-karting (or 'karting', as the professionals like to call it). There are licensed drivers from ages seven to seventy. There are also karting centres, with special tracks built just for go-karts, in most capital cities. They provide the karts, racing equipment and safety gear for anyone wanting to have a go.

Karting is also an internationally recognised sport and is very competitive. Many of the world's greatest Formula One drivers, such as Nigel Mansell and Alain Prost, began their careers kart racing. They perfected their skills kart racing before moving onto other motorsports.

Karting is also a much cheaper motorsport than Formula One.

There are different categories of go-kart too. The first is known as the Super Kart. These karts actually race on the race-car circuits used by Formula One. Super Karts have a big engine and can travel at speeds of up to 260 kilometres per hour. They even have a gearbox, just like a car.

The second type of kart is a Sprint Kart. They have a smaller engine than the Super Kart and no gears. They race on tracks built especially for them; the tracks are usually no longer than a kilometre. And they are narrower than race-car tracks, which means the karts race a lot closer to one another. This makes for an exciting race.

GLOSSARY

Apex

Point where the kart is turning the most sharply.

Back marker

A kart that is running near the back of the field.

Binding

A term used to describe the kart slowing down excessively in the turns, because both rear tyres are planted too firmly on the ground.

Blistering
What happens when racing tyres overheat.

Disqualification
A severe punishment when racing; it can be imposed for ignoring the flags, breaking rules or deliberately damaging another kart.

Flags
Used to communicate with drivers.

Green flag
The signal to start.

Black flag
Means the driver must report to the pit immediately.

Yellow flag
Means 'slow down; there is danger ahead'.

Blue flag with a yellow diagonal

Means that a faster car is approaching, or someone is following close.

Black and white chequered flag

Signals the end of the race.

Grid

Short for 'starting grid'. This is the order in which the drivers line up for the race start. This order is usually determined through qualifying heats.

Hairpin

A sharp 180 degree turn.

Horsepower

A unit of measurement for the power of the engine.

Oversteering

Describes what happens when the kart enters a corner, the rear tyres lose grip before the front tyres, and the rear of the kart slides towards the outside of the corner.

Pit

Area where the kart is taken to refuel, change tyres or be repaired.

Shunt

A crash, or accident.

EQUIPMENT

Clothes

Kart drivers are required to wear purpose-made and approved driving suits or 'leathers', approved safety helmets, gloves and lace-up shoes that cover the ankles.

Karts

Karts are state-of-the-art driving machines, which are about two metres long and 1.2 metres wide, with a base height from the ground of about ten centimetres. They weigh around 100 kilograms and come fitted with auto-transmission gears. They usually have

180 cc engines. Depending on the length of the track, karts can typically be accelerated to speeds of up to 100 kilometres per hour. Considering their low base heights and maximum speeds at this level, kart racing is pretty extreme.

Karts are designed to protect the driver, but accidents can still occur, and safety has to be a top priority.

Specially built tyre barriers around the circuit protect the driver from injury, should they veer off the track.

PHIL KETTLE

Phil Kettle is an award-winning author of more than 200 books. As well as being the author of the *Billy Kool* series, Phil is especially well-known for his *Toocool* series of books.

Phil lives in regional Victoria. He spends his time visiting schools and running around after numerous grandchildren. He grew up on a vineyard, and played football and cricket when he was  young. He loved any sport where he could kick, hit or throw something.

Phil is a popular and sought-after speaker at schools. His presentations and workshops motivate and encourage even the most reluctant writers and readers.

THE XTREME WORLD OF
BILLY KOOL

CPSIA information can be obtained
at www.ICGtesting.com
Printed in the USA
LVHW032341111122
732945LV00047B/3955

9 781925 308754